The One That Got Away

For Ben—P.E.
To Cristina & Tona—D.Z.

Clarion Books
a Houghton Mifflin Company imprint
215 Park Avenue South, New York, NY 10003
Text copyright © 1992 by Percival Everett
Illustrations copyright © 1992 by Dirk Zimmer

Printed in the U.S.A.

Library of Congress Cataloging-in-Publication Data

Everett, Percival L.
The one that got away / by Percival Everett ;
illustrated by Dirk Zimmer.
p.   cm.
Summary: Three cowhands chase and corral ones in this zany
book about the Wild West.
ISBN 0-395-56437-9
[1. Cowboys—Fiction.   2. One (The number)—Fiction.]
I. Zimmer, Dirk, ill.   II. Title.
PZ7.E9190n   1992
[E]—dc20   91-8333   CIP   AC
WOZ 10 9 8 7 6 5 4 3 2 1

The One That Got Away

By Percival Everett ▲ Illustrated by Dirk Zimmer

CLARION BOOKS · NEW YORK

On the first day out,
much to their surprise,
they caught one.

It was a strong one
and it fought hard
against the ropes.

But they held it
and wrestled it into the corral.
"Boy, howdy, we caught us
a good one," they said.

They did not dilly-dally.
They went looking for
another one.

They looked in the canyon.
They looked near the waterhole.

Then they saw one.
And another
and a big one.
It was a herd.

They rode into the herd
and threw hoolies over one,
then another, until they
had captured many.

They put the new ones
in the corral with
the first one.

Then, on a night when
the moon was full,
one jumped the fence
and got away.

In the morning,
they counted and discovered
that one was missing.
"Oh my," they said.
"We've lost the biggest one."

So they rode out
to look for the one
that got away.

They looked in the canyon.
They looked near the waterhole.
Then they found tracks
and they followed them.

They saw the big one
on top of a mountain.
The mountain was very steep,
but there were stairs.

They started the climb
up to the top.

Partway up, a stair was missing.
"Oh dear," they said,
looking around.
"We must find a stair."

23

They decided which of them
should go back down the mountain,
and he took off like a shot.

He went to a hole in the ground
and dropped down
the loop of his lariat.

He pulled up a stair.
It was a stairwell.

He took the stair
back up the mountain
and they put it in place.

Finally, they reached the top,
but no one was there.

On the way home,
they talked about
the ones that were left.
"We have eight," they said.

But when they reached
the corral...

they had not
a single one.